The Indigo Jackal

A Tale from India
Retold by Frances Bacon
Illustrated by Helen Bacon

India

Vijay lives in New Delhi, the capital of India. He lives with his mother and father, his little brother, and his grandparents. Vijay loves the Indian stories his grandmother tells.

This story from India reminds us not to turn our back on our friends and teaches us the importance of loyalty.

loyalty being faithful

Long, long ago in India, there lived a very foolish jackal. His name was Raji. Raji lived with a pack of jackals and had many friends, but he longed to be different. He wanted to be better than the other jackals. In fact, Raji's dream was to be king of the jungle!

jungle an area of land that is thickly covered
        with tropical trees and vines

One day, Raji was wandering around
the edge of a village, looking for food.
   At the first house, he found some meat
left out to dry in the sun. Raji gobbled it up.

At the second house, he found a bowl of
curry left to cool on a windowsill. Raji gobbled
it up, too.

Raji's stomach was now very full, but he was greedy as well as foolish. So he went on to the third house.

This house belonged to the village artist. Behind the house stood a large tub of indigo dye. Raji thought the tub might be full of tasty treats, so he jumped in.

The tub was deep, and Raji swam around for some time before he was able to climb out and run back to the jungle.

indigo a dark violet–blue color

As he ran, Raji saw that his legs were bright indigo. He turned in a circle to look at his tail. His tail was indigo, too!

Raji howled in surprise and raced to the stream. He splashed and splashed, but he could not wash off the dye. Raji's yellow coat was now a beautiful indigo!

At first, Raji was worried that the other jackals would laugh at him. So he came up with a plan to fool them all.

When the pack of jackals came down to the stream to drink, they saw Raji sitting on the highest rock. Before they could say a word, Raji began to speak.

"The goddess of the jungle has chosen me to be your king," he said. "She has given me a beautiful indigo coat. This special color shows that I am king. From this day on, I shall rule everyone in the jungle."

The jackals saw that Raji was a very beautiful color. They bowed low and cheered, "Long live King Raji!"

The birds flew around Raji's head. They chirped loudly, saying, "Long live King Raji!"

The other animals of the jungle heard
the chirping of the birds. They came to see
the new king for themselves.

"Your coat is indeed beautiful, King Raji,"
they said. "We will follow you."

The foolish jackal loved being king.
He enjoyed being different and special.

Raji gave the lions and tigers important jobs, and they became his new friends. He **assigned** the elephants to be his guards. No animal was allowed to speak to Raji without first gaining permission from the elephants.

assigned given a task or duty

Raji believed that he was better than the other animals of the jungle, but he had one problem. Every time he saw his old jackal friends, he knew that underneath the indigo dye was his old, yellow coat. He was not really a king. He was only a jackal.

Raji worried that the other animals would find out his secret. So he sent all the other jackals out of the jungle. Standing on the highest rock, the indigo jackal watched as the other jackals left their home.

As he turned to go, the oldest jackal spoke to Raji. "How can you send your friends away, Raji? Is friendship not important to you?"

"Old jackal, you are no friend of the king," Raji replied cruelly.

friendship making and keeping friends

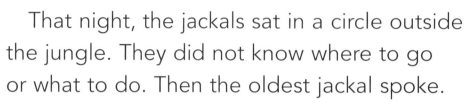

That night, the jackals sat in a circle outside
the jungle. They did not know where to go
or what to do. Then the oldest jackal spoke.

"Raji has treated us badly," he said. "We
know that he is not special. We know that
he does not deserve the respect of the lions,
the tigers, and the other animals of the jungle.
I have a plan that will show him up for what
he really is—just another jackal."

As the moon rose in the sky, the jackal pack
threw back their heads and began to howl
as only jackals can.

From high on his rock, Raji heard the howls. So, too, did his elephant guards and his new friends, the lions and the tigers.

Raji tried to keep quiet, but it was very hard. He was, after all, just a foolish jackal who had fallen into a tub of indigo dye.

Finally, Raji could stand it no longer. He threw back his head and howled at the moon. The other animals could not believe their ears.

"Raji is no king," they said. "He is only a strange-colored jackal! Even worse, he is a jackal who has turned his back on his friends!"

Some people say that the lions and tigers killed the indigo jackal for being an impostor. Other people say that the animals chased him far, far away. Nobody really knows what became of Raji. However, the jackal pack went back to the jungle, and the foolish jackal was never seen again.

impostor   someone who cheats or tricks others by pretending
            to be someone or something they are not

Discussion Starters

1 Raji is described as "a very foolish jackal." Why do you think he is called "foolish?"

2 Turning your back on your friends is usually a mistake. How should you treat your friends?

How could Raji's life have turned out differently if he had been loyal to his friends?